ENGINEERING CHALLENGES

BUILDING DAMS

by Nikole Brooks Bethea

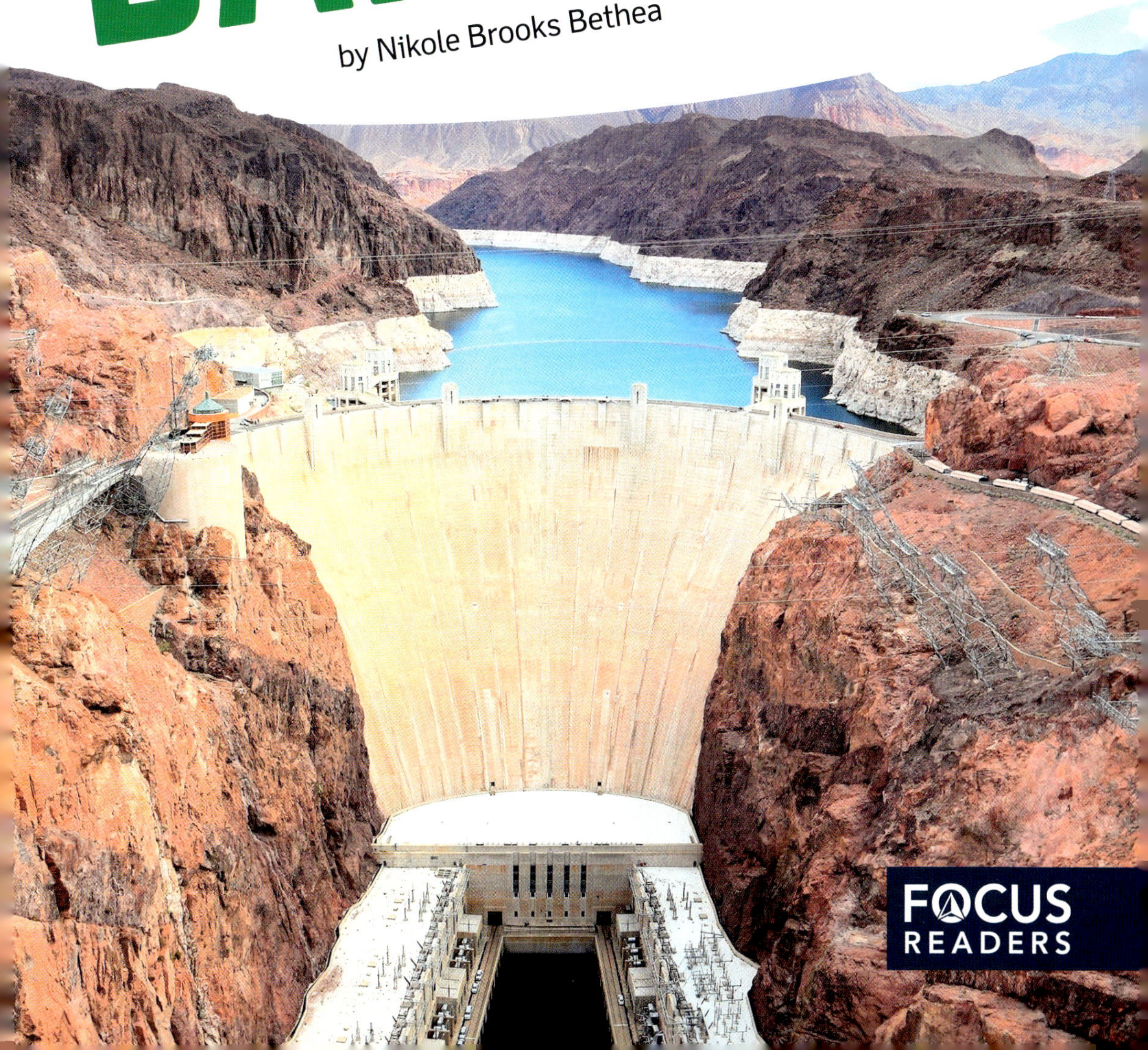

FOCUS READERS

FOCUS READERS

WWW.FOCUSREADERS.COM

Focus Readers is distributed by North Star Editions:
sales@northstareditions.com | 888-417-0195

Produced for Focus Readers by Red Line Editorial.

Content Consultant: Omid Mohseni, PhD, PE; Senior Water Resources Engineer at Barr Engineering Co.; Adjunct Associate Professor, Department of Civil, Environmental and Geo-Engineering, University of Minnesota

Photographs ©: Tupungato/Shutterstock Images, cover, 1; pkujiahe/iStockphoto, 4–5; holbox/Shutterstock Images, 7; poplasen/iStockphoto, 9; irakite/Shutterstock Images, 10–11; ventdusud/iStockphoto, 13; deldew/iStockphoto, 15; toddmedia/iStockphoto, 16; AP Images, 18–19; nesneJkraM/iStockphoto, 21; lfreytag/iStockphoto, 22–23; Red Line Editorial, 24–25, 27, 29

ISBN
978-1-63517-252-2 (hardcover)
978-1-63517-317-8 (paperback)
978-1-63517-447-2 (ebook pdf)
978-1-63517-382-6 (hosted ebook)

Library of Congress Control Number: 2017935925

Printed in the United States of America
Mankato, MN
June, 2017

ABOUT THE AUTHOR

Nikole Brooks Bethea is the author of more than 20 nonfiction books for children. Her background includes bachelor's and master's degrees in environmental engineering. She is a licensed professional engineer. She uses her engineering background to pique children's interest in science and engineering topics.

TABLE OF CONTENTS

CHAPTER 1

AWESOME POWER

Han stood in awe in front of the Three Gorges Dam in China. The dam was more than 600 feet (183 m) tall. It was more than 1.3 miles (2.1 km) long. Powerful floodwaters emerged from the dam. Most impressive, though, was the dam's ability to generate energy. It is the largest **hydroelectric** plant in the world.

The Three Gorges Dam spans the Yangtze River in central China.

Water is necessary for people to survive, and people have always tried to control it. Dams achieve this goal. They are built across a river or stream to block the flow of water. This creates a **reservoir**, or lake, behind the dam.

Outlets allow people to release the water downstream in a controlled way. This water might be needed for crop **irrigation** or drinking water. Or it might simply supply downstream flow.

One of the earliest dams was built in ancient Egypt around 3000 BCE. The dam protected the capital city from the Nile River's flooding. The Roman Empire also built dams. Two of them are still used

The Romans built the Proserpina Dam in Spain in the first or second century CE.

today. Both are in Spain. They were built during the first and second centuries CE.

In the past, people built dams for flood control and irrigation. Ancient Roman dams had openings at the bottom. These released floodwater downstream.

The dams also had gates that could be opened. This supplied irrigation water from the reservoir.

Many ancient dams lacked **spillways**. Therefore, when water flowed over the top of the dams during large floods, the dams often failed. Modern dam designs include spillways. They allow large volumes of floodwater to pass over the dam or bypass it. This keeps the dam structure from being damaged.

Today, most dams are designed so they can generate energy. This is known as hydroelectric energy. The process begins when water reaches an area at the bottom of a dam. Flowing water has a

Many modern dams have spillways and produce electricity.

lot of power. This water turns the blades of a turbine. The turbine shaft extends into a generator, causing it to spin. The generator produces electricity.

CHAPTER 2

DESIGNING A DAM

There are two basic types of dams: **concrete** dams and earthen dams. Concrete dams can be arch dams, gravity dams, buttress dams, or a combination. Earthen dams are large walls of earth or stone called **embankments**. Each type has a different design. And each type of dam can serve a different purpose.

The Aldeadávila Dam is a concrete arch-gravity dam between Spain and Portugal.

An arch dam is curved. The arched shape resists the force of water pushing on the dam. Arch dams are thinner than other types of dams. Therefore, less material is required to build them.

Gravity dams stop the flow of water with their own weight. These massive dams are expensive to build. That's because they use large amounts of concrete.

Buttress dams are gravity dams with supports called buttresses. They can have a flat or curved face. Triangular supports are spaced along the back, or downstream side, of buttress dams. There are open spaces between the buttresses.

Buttresses help support the Roselend Dam in France.

As a result, these dams use less material than gravity dams.

Earthen dams are constructed of natural materials such as earth or rock. They often have a center core that is waterproof. The core might be made of clay or concrete. This prevents water from passing through the dam. These dams hold back water with their own weight.

Dam engineers must consider many factors. First they must decide what type of dam to build. **Topography** is the main factor that determines this. A stream running through a deep canyon with rocky walls requires a different design than a stream flowing through low, rolling hills. The geology of the site also determines the type of dam that can be built. The rock and soil must provide a good **foundation** for the dam.

During the design process, engineers study the forces acting on the dam. A dam must withstand the pressure the water applies on its upstream face. Dams must also withstand uplift pressure. This

Water flows through the Katse Dam in Lesotho, a small country in southern Africa.

is an upward pressure from water seeping into the dam's openings and into the joint between the dam and its foundation. Engineers must also calculate how temperature changes will affect the dam.

A dam was built on the North River to create Lake Tuscaloosa in Alabama.

For example, water grows bigger when it turns to ice. Plus, engineers must consider the weight of the dam itself.

In addition, engineers must think about environmental and **ecological** changes that dams can cause. For instance, how will the change from flowing water to standing water affect the local wildlife?

ENGINEERING DESIGN PROCESS

Engineers must be confident in their plans. They use various codes, models, and tools in their planning. This ensures a dam will be strong enough.

ASK: What type of dam should be built at this location?

IMAGINE: Brainstorm the positive and negative aspects of each type of dam. How strong is the dam? How will it affect the environment? Choose the best type for this location.

PLAN: Draw a diagram of the selected dam design. Write a list of materials needed.

CREATE: Develop a computer model of the dam design. Input relevant forces, flood stages of the river, and rainfall data.

IMPROVE: What worked? What didn't work? Modify the design and retest.

CHAPTER 3

CREATIVE SOLUTIONS

The Hoover Dam is a giant concrete arch-gravity dam on the border between Nevada and Arizona. Building it was a huge, complex job.

Before the first concrete could be poured, the site had to be dry. That meant the entire flow of the Colorado River had to be routed around the construction site.

Workers build Hoover Dam, then known as Boulder Dam, in 1934.

Engineers blasted four large tunnels through the canyon walls. Drilling rigs made holes in the rock face. Workers then filled the holes with dynamite and blasted. One ton (907 kg) of dynamite was fired for every 14 feet (4.3 m) of tunnel. The tunnels were completed in November 1932. Then, workers dumped rock and earth into the river to block its flow. The river began flowing through the four tunnels.

Engineers faced another challenge. Heat is produced as concrete is mixed. The concrete shrinks and cracks as it cools. Hoover Dam was to be 726 feet (221 m) tall. It would be 660 feet (201 m)

Hoover Dam is a National Historic Landmark.

thick at the base and 45 feet (13.7 m) thick at the top. All of this concrete would take 125 years to cool if poured all together. So engineers poured it into small blocks. Then they placed pipes within the blocks. Cold water ran through the pipes to cool the concrete. Hoover Dam was completed in March 1936.

GRAND COULEE DAM

Grand Coulee Dam was finished in 1941 on the Columbia River in Washington. The gravity dam created Lake Roosevelt. At 550 feet (168 m) high and 5,223 feet (1,592 m) long, the dam is the largest concrete structure and the largest hydroelectric producer in the United States. It contains nearly 12 million cubic yards (9.2 million cubic m) of concrete. That's enough to build a highway from Seattle, Washington, to Miami, Florida. Each year, the dam's plant produces more than 21 billion kilowatt-hours of electricity. That can power 2.3 million homes for a year.

In addition to producing electricity, the Grand Coulee Dam helps with irrigation and flood control.

CHAPTER 4

ENGINEERING CHALLENGE

In this activity, you become the engineer. You will construct a dam in the corner of an aluminum pan.

Materials:

You'll need a baking pan, a cup of water, and materials to build a dam. Options include modeling clay, craft sticks, clips, cardboard, and rocks or gravel.

Modeling clay and a paper plate can combine to make a simple but effective gravity dam.

Procedure:

Pretend a river is coming in from the corner of the pan. Without a proper dam, the river will flood the whole pan. It's your job to build a corner dam that will hold the water back.

1. Consider the four different dam types: gravity, buttress, embankment, and arch. Which one will be the simplest to make?
2. Use your materials to build the dam. Modeling clay works well for a simple embankment dam. Make sure to put the clay in a strong shape. Seal all the holes.

You can create a simple earthen embankment dam using modeling clay.

3. Pour water into the corner of the pan. What happened? Was your dam able to hold back the water?

Improve It!

- How did your materials hold up? Could they be more effective if you used them differently?

- Do you think another construction material would work better than the one you used for a particular type of dam?
- Now that you've built a simple dam, try building one that's even stronger. Which type of dam might work best with your materials?
- Pour out the water and dry the pan. Recreate your dam using different materials. Test it out. Does it hold better or worse than the first design?
- Are there ways you could make your dam even stronger by combining different types of dams? For example, you could add an arch

Adding craft-stick buttresses to this gravity dam made it even stronger.

shape. What about adding buttresses to strengthen your dam?

- Pour out the water and keep trying. See how tall you can build a dam without it leaking into the center area.

FOCUS ON

BUILDING DAMS

Write your answers on a separate piece of paper.

1. Write a paragraph explaining the main ideas of Chapter 2.

2. Which of the four types of dams would be most difficult to build? Why?

3. What material is used to build an embankment dam?

   A. rock
   B. rubber
   C. metal

4. After a dam is built on a river, what might happen to homes located upstream?

   A. The river in front of the homes might dry up.
   B. The homes might have less access to electricity.
   C. The river might flood the homes.

Answer key on page 32.

GLOSSARY

concrete
A strong, stonelike material made from gravel, sand, cement, and water.

ecological
Relating to the relationship between living organisms and their environment.

embankments
Walls of earth or stone.

foundation
The supporting base of a structure.

hydroelectric
Relating to the generation of electricity with flowing water.

irrigation
The redirecting of water to help crops grow.

reservoir
A human-made lake used for water supply storage.

spillways
Passages for excess water from a dam.

topography
The features of the earth's surface.

TO LEARN MORE

BOOKS

Latham, Donna. *Canals and Dams: Investigate Feats of Engineering*. White River Junction, VT: Nomad Press, 2013.

Miller, Heather. *The Hoover Dam*. Chicago: Norwood House Press, 2014.

Nagelhout, Ryan. *How Do Dams Work?* New York: PowerKids Press, 2016.

NOTE TO EDUCATORS

Visit **www.focusreaders.com** to find lesson plans, activities, links, and other resources related to this title.

INDEX

Answer Key: 1. Answers will vary; **2.** Answers will vary; **3.** A; **4.** C